To John and Kaye Lindauer —E.S.

To good neighbor Dan —M.P.

THIS IS A BORZOI BOOK PUBLISHED BY ALFRED A. KNOPF

Text copyright © 2012 by Eileen Spinelli
Jacket art and interior illustrations copyright © 2012 by Marjorie Priceman

Visit us on the Web! randomhouse.com/kids

Educators and librarians, for a variety of teaching tools, visit us at randomhouse.com/teachers

Library of Congress Cataloging-in-Publication Data
Spinelli, Eileen.
Cold snap / by Eileen Spinelli ; illustrated by Marjorie Priceman.
p.   cm.
Summary: A cold snap has everyone in the town of Toby Mills feeling down,
until the mayor's wife thinks of a way to warm things up again.
ISBN 978-0-375-85700-3 (trade) — ISBN 978-0-375-95700-0 (lib. bdg.)
[1. Cold—Fiction. 2. Community life—Fiction.] I. Priceman, Marjorie, ill. II. Title.
PZ7.S7566Cns 2012
[E]—dc22
2011013290

The text of this book is set in 14-point Goudy.
The illustrations were created using gouache on watercolor paper.

MANUFACTURED IN CHINA
October 2012
10 9 8 7 6 5 4 3 2 1

First Edition

Cold Snap

BY EILEEN SPINELLI

ILLUSTRATED BY MARJORIE PRICEMAN

ALFRED A. KNOPF • NEW YORK

It was snowy cold in Toby Mills.

Ears tingled.

Cheeks were frosty pink.

Toes, too numb to wiggle.

An icicle dangled from the nose of the statue
of General Toby—the town's founder.

After school, Millie Moffat made snow angels.
Her little brother, Chip, threw snowballs—*splat!*—
at the general's hat.

Franky Tornetta whooshed down T-Bone Hill—*whomp!*—
right into Stix Hartman's snowman.

Millie twirled Chip round and round until they both toppled
into a snowbank.

By nightfall, the kids of Toby Mills were dragging. And wet. And shivering.

And so they trooped home—boots crunching on snowy streets—ready for hot chocolate and flannel pajamas.

ON SATURDAY, the icicle on General Toby's nose reached down to the dimple on his chin.

Ice glazed alleyways.

Spoken words became puffballs in the frigid air.

Page one of the *Toby Mills Crier* read: COLD SNAP!

The Sullivan sisters served steamy soup and bubbling stew at the Sullivan Diner.

In between customers, they knitted mittens as big as flapjacks for all the kids in Toby Mills.

Mrs. Moffat—the church soloist—gargled with salt water every hour to avoid getting a sore throat.

ON SUNDAY, General Toby's icicle hung past his chin.

The Moffats and the Sullivan sisters slogged through the slush to church.

Mrs. Moffat sipped lemony tea from a thermos before her solo.

Millie and Chip huddle-cuddled close to Elijah, the church cat.

Pastor Pickthorn—teeth chattering—preached in earmuffs and overcoat.

The Sullivan sisters wore long underwear under their dresses.

MONDAY WAS EVEN COLDER.

And the general's icicle was growing.

Franky Tornetta pulled Miss Dove, the teacher, across the frozen parking lot on his sled.

Stix Hartman—slipping and sliding—carried her books.

The mayor's office fielded complaints about the weather.

Street workers made fires in metal drums.

Mr. Moffat was stuck on a city train for two hours after the doors froze shut.

He and the other passengers had to be rescued through windows by firefighters.

TUESDAY WAS COLDER STILL.

General Toby's icicle touched the medal on his chest.

Pastor Pickthorn's furnace had gone out during the night. When he stepped from his bed on Tuesday morning, his bare feet nearly froze to the floor.

His dog, Mugs, begged for his fuzzy red coat—the one he had balked at wearing before.

The Sullivan sisters knitted a sweater for Elijah.

Millie Moffat tossed sunflower seeds to the birds,
who were braving the winter.

ON WEDNESDAY, the temperature plunged even lower, and so did General Toby's icicle.

A bitter wind nipped at noses. Tipped trash cans.

Flipped Chip off the creaky schoolyard swing.

Franky Tornetta stopped whining about his itchy woolen socks and put on three pairs.

The Toby Mills Movie Theater had a problem with its furnace.
Tickets were now half price and bring-your-own-blanket.

There were more complaints to the mayor, who stayed overtime at
City Hall.

His wife brought him his toasty pink bunny slippers. And his warm
blue bathrobe, which he wore over his suit.

Mrs. Moffat didn't have to coax Chip to take a warm bath.

At bedtime, Millie Moffat tucked her cold feet into her flapjack-y
mittens.

TOBY M

LONG HOT SUMMER
7:00
LITTLE MISS SUNSHI
9:00
B. Y. O. B.

BY 8 A.M. ON THURSDAY MORNING, the official thermometer outside City Hall fell to a number it had never met before—*zero!*

If the people hadn't been so cold, they might have cheered.

General Toby's icicle reached his belly button.

Mr. Moffat danced a jig to keep warm till his train arrived.

Miss Dove brought shells and a beach chair and a plastic seagull to class. "Imagine it's summer," she told her students.

Pastor Pickthorn taped two hot-water bottles onto his feet for his afternoon nap.

Mrs. Moffat discovered a nest of mice in her oven. She didn't have the heart to chase the little critters into the terrible chill— so she baked her husband's birthday cake at the Sullivan Diner.

BY FRIDAY, out-of-towners were calling Toby Mills
"the new North Pole."

The tip of General Toby's fat icicle kissed the ground.

"Something must be done!" declared the mayor.

"I have an idea," said the mayor's wife.

And she did.

All day long, the mayor's staff delivered flyers.

*WINTER
SURPRISE!*

*T-Bone Hill
7 p.m.*

*Everybody
Welcome!*

"Winter surprise?" groaned Miss Dove. "I was planning to cuddle in bed with a book."

"Winter surprise?" snorted Mr. Moffat. "I have a surprise for the mayor. By seven p.m., we'll all be Popsicles."

"Now, now," said Mrs. Moffat. "We ought to go. It's our civic duty."

And so they went—the citizens of Toby Mills—to T-Bone Hill.

The sky was dark and clear. The moon was silver as sleet.

But look! There, on the hilltop . . .

. . . a soaring, roaring bonfire.

Sparks flew into the night like newborn
stars. But most happily of all was something that
Toby Mills had missed for a week—heat! Warm,
old-fashioned, where-have-you-been heat.

The mayor ladled cups of hot cider from steaming pots.

The mayor's staff served doughnuts.

Stix Hartman played a lively tune on his kazoo.

Mrs. Moffat sang. So did Mugs and Elijah.

Mr. Moffat joined the Sullivan sisters in a dance.

Pastor Pickthorn practiced Sunday's sermon on the mayor's wife.

Miss Dove demonstrated how to make sugar-on-snow candy.

First, she sent Franky Tornetta to a nearby snowbank with a big bowl and a spoon.

Millie and Chip filled the bowl with clean snow.

When they returned, Miss Dove drizzled hot maple syrup over the snow. It hardened into the best candy anyone at Toby Mills had ever tasted.

Everyone had such a warm and cozy time that they forgot all about the cold snap.

The next morning, when they woke
up, the sun was bright and the snow
was melting and the icicle on General
Toby's nose had shattered at his feet.

The thermometer outside City Hall
read 15° F . . .

and was heading up!

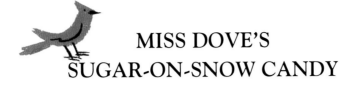

MISS DOVE'S
SUGAR-ON-SNOW CANDY

INGREDIENTS:

Real maple syrup

Fresh, clean snow

Boil real maple syrup to 250° F (adults only, please).

Scoop clean (very clean!) snow into a large bowl (a good job for kids).

Drizzle hot maple syrup lightly over the snow (adults, please).

Pass out forks. Eat the sticky top layer with a fork (everyone!).

NOTE: Some people follow the candy with a bite of sour pickle or a saltine cracker or a doughnut.